F

M

N

FEB

X

Nine Candles

by *Maria Testa*
illustrated by
Amanda Schaffer

Carolrhoda Books, Inc./Minneapolis

This book was made possible, in part, by a Barbara Karlin Grant from the Society of Children's Book Writers and Illustrators.

—M.T.

For their modeling help and inspiration, my gratitude and many thanks to Melissa Austin, Sergio Cabrera, and Robbie Gonzales—a very special boy who made the pictures come alive! Also, thank you to my parents, Albert and Lillian, and to family and friends for being there.

—A.S.

Carolrhoda Books, Inc. c/o The Lerner Group
241 First Avenue North, Minneapolis, MN 55401

LIBRARY OF CONGRESS CATALOGING-IN-PUBLICATION DATA

Testa, Maria.
   Nine Candles/by Maria Testa; illustrated by Amanda Schaffer.
   p. cm.
   Summary: After visiting his mother in prison on his seventh birthday, Raymond wishes it were his ninth birthday when Mama has promised to be home with his dad and him.
   ISBN 0-87614-940-9
   [1. Mothers and sons—Fiction. 2. Prisoners—Fiction. 3. Birthdays—Fiction.] I. Schaffer, Amanda, ill. II. Title.
PZ7.T2877Ni 1996
[Fic]—dc20   95-16575
                                                   CIP
                                                   AC

Manufactured in the United States of America
1 2 3 4 5 6 – JR – 01 00 99 98 97 96

For my husband, Greg, with love
—M.T.

To children who must overcome family
struggles that life sometimes brings
—A.S.

*T*oday is Sunday, my favorite day. I get up early and see the sun getting up, too. I want the day to last a long, long time.

Sunday is the day Dad and I visit Mama.

This Sunday is extra special—I'm seven years old today. I stand in front of my bedroom mirror.

"Happy birthday," I say out loud.

It's good to be seven. But more than anything in the world, I want to be nine.

Dad knocks on the door and comes into my room.

"Happy birthday, Raymond!" he says. "You're up early."

"I want to see Mama," I say. "Let's leave right now."

But Dad reminds me that we can't visit Mama until ten o'clock. He helps me choose special clothes to wear. I want to look nice for Mama today.

"I hope Mama remembers my birthday," I say. Dad doesn't say anything.

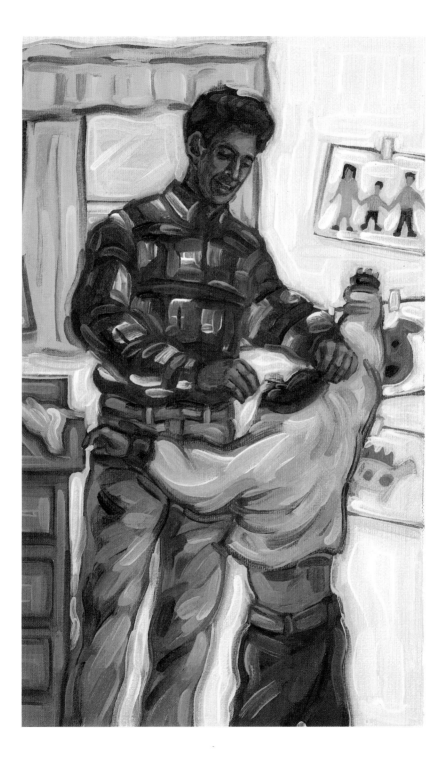

Dad and I have breakfast together. Then he puts three presents on the table.

"I wish I could give you more, Raymond," he says, "but . . . you know."

I know. We haven't had much money since Mama went away.

I open my presents. They're fantastic! Dad got me a set of watercolor paints and brushes, a thick pad of paper, and a soccer ball.

"Come on, Dad," I say. "Let's go outside and kick the ball around."

Playing soccer makes the time go faster. It feels good to kick the ball hard and far.

It's fun playing outside with Dad. But we used to have even more fun when Mama was here.

Pretty soon, Dad says it's time to go.

The bus ride is long. We travel through the city, past all the tall buildings. We travel through the suburbs. There are a lot of baseball fields.

Then we are in the country. Green grass is everywhere.

The cows in the fields watch our bus drive by. I wave at them, like I do every Sunday. The cows swish their tails.

"I think they recognize me," I say to Dad. He thinks so, too.

"Hey, cows," I whisper. "Today's my birthday."

Finally, the bus stops in front of the place where Mama is staying. There's a big sign out front—State Correctional Facility. Dad says it's just a long name for a prison. Mama's had to stay here ever since the larceny. She used to work at a restaurant, but she took a lot of money that wasn't hers.

Mama says she made a mistake. She says she was wrong to take that money, even though Dad was out of a job at the time. She says she's never been so sorry for anything in her whole life. I don't like what she did, but I believe her.

Every time I see that big prison sign, I get a cold feeling in my stomach, like I just ate too much ice cream. But I can't wait to see Mama.

I grab Dad's hand and lead him through the prison gates.

Dad looks at me and shakes his head. "You surprise me, Raymond," he says. "I never thought you'd like to come here so much."

I never thought I would, either. It's hard to explain, but I try.

"I hate this prison," I say. "I hate it more than anything. But I love Mama and I love to visit her, even here."

There are two buildings at the prison. The big one is for men, and the little one, up on a hill, is for women. The fences surrounding both buildings are almost as high as the sky. There are people in brown uniforms everywhere. Some of them have guns, and some have dogs.

Dad and I don't talk to any of them. We go inside the little building.

The line in the waiting room is long. At first I don't recognize anyone, but then I see Tony and his grandmother. Tony is my friend.

"Happy birthday, Raymond," Tony says, and I give him a high five. Tony's a great friend—he remembered my birthday! I used to think he was lucky because he's already nine. But Tony says he'd give anything in the world to be eleven.

We reach the front of the line. It's our turn to walk through the metal detector. I used to think it was kind of cool, but not anymore. Last Sunday Dad wore a belt with a big buckle, and the metal detector made a loud beeping noise. The guard told Dad to step aside, and then two other guards searched him all over. I got really scared, because I thought the guards might take Dad down the hill to the big building and keep him there. But they didn't. They just talked to Dad for a minute, and then everything was okay.

Dad's not wearing a belt today. The metal detector doesn't make a sound.

Next we have to wait for the automatic doors. The first one opens, and we step inside. Then it closes behind us. There's a second door in front of us, and I hold Dad's hand while we wait for it to open. I'm glad when it does.

Dad puts his hand on my head and messes up my hair.

"How're you doing, buddy?" he asks.

"I'm okay," I say.

Dad smiles a sad smile. I smile, too. Dad understands.

We finally make it to the visiting room. It's really crowded. There are lots of tables and chairs everywhere. Dad and I sit down and wait for Mama.

"Where is she?" I ask. I'm sitting on the edge of my seat.

"She'll be here," Dad says. "Be patient." But I don't want to be patient.

"I hope Mama remembers my birthday," I say.

Dad puts his arm around me. "I hope so, too."

There she is! I see Mama at the same time she sees me. We run to each other, and I jump into her arms.

Dad wraps his arms around us both. We don't talk for a long time.

We sit down at our table. Mama is the first to speak.

"You look handsome today, Raymond," she says. "How are you?"

"Fine," I say.

"How's school?" Mama asks.

"Fine." I look over at Dad. Why doesn't Mama wish me a happy birthday? Did she forget?

Suddenly, a guard calls out Mama's name. Mama turns around and nods her head.

"I have to leave for a minute," Mama says. "But I'll be back soon." She gets up and follows the guard out of the visiting room.

"Dad!" I cry. "What's going on? Why did Mama have to leave? Is she in trouble? She hasn't even said happy birthday!"

Dad shakes his head and shrugs his shoulders. He looks tired as he slowly scans the room. All of a sudden his eyes get big. "Raymond!" he says, pointing across the room. "Look!"

Mama and the guard are walking toward our table. They're both smiling and looking right at me.

Mama is carrying a cake, a chocolate cake, my favorite cake in the whole world. She remembered! It's my birthday cake, and Mama puts it down in front of me. I look up at her and smile. Then I take a deep breath and blow out all seven candles.

Mama and Dad sing "Happy Birthday," and then everyone around us joins in. My face gets really hot, but I get up and give Mama a big hug.

"Wow! I can't believe you remembered," I whisper into her ear.

"Of course I did, Raymond," Mama whispers back. "I love you too much to forget your birthday."

The guard cuts the cake into small pieces, and we share it with lots of people I don't even know. Mama looks kind of sad. I know she wishes she were cutting my cake. But only the guard is allowed to use the knife. It's still the best birthday cake I've ever had. Dad and Mama watch me eat, and they both smile.

"You're getting so big," Mama says. I'm proud that she has noticed. "But don't get too big too soon," she adds.

"I won't, Mama," I say. "I'll wait for you."

We finish the cake, and I tell Mama all about the presents Dad gave me.

"I'll make a watercolor painting just for you, Mama," I promise. "I'll give it to you next Sunday."

"I can't wait," she says. Then she reaches one hand out to Dad and one to me. We sit there quietly, all holding hands.

"I miss you both so much," Mama says.

A woman in a brown uniform steps into the center of the visiting room. I recognize her. I don't like her at all. "Visiting time is over!" she calls out in a very loud voice.

"No!" I shout back even louder. I am mad. All of a sudden, I don't care about watercolors and soccer balls and chocolate birthday cakes. I just want Mama to be at home with Dad and me.

Mama holds me tightly. "I'm sorry, Raymond," she whispers. "I'm so very, very sorry."

"I want you to come home," I cry. "When can you come home?"

Mama wipes away my tears. Dad puts his arm around her shoulders. "Oh, Raymond," she says softly, "you know when." One by one Mama picks up my seven birthday candles. She presses them into my hand.

"When there are nine candles on your birthday cake," Mama says. "I promise I will be home when there are nine candles on your birthday cake."

The bus ride home seems shorter. It's dark, too dark to see the cows or the baseball fields.

I'm tired.

When the bus stops in front of our building, I climb onto Dad's back, and he carries me upstairs to our apartment.

"It's been a long, long day, Raymond. But it was good," Dad says. "Sweet dreams," he whispers, as he tucks me into bed. I slip my seven birthday candles under my pillow.

"I only have one dream," I say. "Just one."

"I know," Dad says. "It's my only dream, too." He kisses me goodnight and turns off the light. I close my eyes and dream my one dream.

Mama is carrying a cake, a chocolate cake, my favorite cake in the whole world. She remembered! It's my birthday cake, and Mama puts it down in front of me. I look up at her and smile. Then I take a deep breath and blow out all nine candles.

Author's Note

Raymond's story is not unusual. At least one and a half million children in the United States currently have a mother or father in prison.

Like Raymond's mother, most women are imprisoned for nonviolent, property-related crimes, and receive an average sentence of two years. Raymond is lucky that he is one of the ten percent of children cared for by their fathers during this time. Half of the children whose mothers are in prison are cared for by grandparents or other relatives, while many are placed in foster care.

Raymond is also lucky that he gets to visit his mother every week. People aren't always imprisoned close to home. The cost of transportation alone keeps many children from visiting regularly.

Having a parent in prison is a lot like being separated from them for other reasons, such as divorce, military service, or illness. It is important that the children of imprisoned parents do not feel alone and that they see their parent as often as possible. It also helps if they stay active in school and keep up with social activities.

Family members, neighbors, teachers, and professionals can supply a lot of support. But adults are not the only people who can help. If you know someone—a classmate, a neighbor, a teammate—whose mother or father is in prison, you have the most important job of all. You can be a friend.